# THE OLD MAN AND THE AFTERNOON CAT

## To librarians, parents, and teachers:

*The Old Man and the Afternoon Cat* is a Parents Magazine READ ALOUD Original — one title in a series of colorfully illustrated and fun-to-read stories that young readers will be sure to come back to time and time again.

Now, in this special school and library edition of *The Old Man and the Afternoon Cat,* adults have an even greater opportunity to increase children's responsiveness to reading and learning — and to have fun every step of the way.

When you finish this story, check the special section at the back of the book. There you will find games, projects, things to talk about, and other educational activities designed to make reading enjoyable by giving children and adults a chance to play together, work together, and talk over the story they have just read.

# I HATE BIRTHDAYS

## by The Old Man

Medium

I HATE BIRTHDAYS, I HATE SPRING. I HATE AL-MOST EV'-RY-THING.

I CAN BE NAS-TY, MEAN AND GRUMPY. I LIKE TO SLEEP ON A BED THAT'S LUMPY.

I'M ALL A-LONE, THERE'S NO ONE BUT ME. NO ONE THAT I THINK A-BOUT, NO ONE THAT I SEE.

NO ONE TO ASK ME, "HOW WAS YOUR DAY?" I'M ALL A-LONE AND I LIKE IT THAT WAY!

**For a free color catalog describing Gareth Stevens' list of high-quality books, call 1-800-341-3569 (USA) or 1-800-461-9120 (Canada).**

**Parents Magazine READ ALOUD Originals:**

Golly Gump Swallowed a Fly
The Housekeeper's Dog
Who Put the Pepper in the Pot?
Those Terrible Toy-Breakers
The Ghost in Dobbs Diner
The Biggest Shadow in the Zoo
The Old Man and the Afternoon Cat
Septimus Bean and His Amazing Machine
Sherlock Chick's First Case
A Garden for Miss Mouse
Witches Four
Bread and Honey

Pigs in the House
Milk and Cookies
But No Elephants
No Carrots for Harry!
Snow Lion
Henry's Awful Mistake
The Fox with Cold Feet
Get Well, Clown-Arounds!
Pets I Wouldn't Pick
Sherlock Chick and the Giant
    Egg Mystery

**Library of Congress Cataloging-in-Publication Data**

Muntean, Michaela.
    The old man and the afternoon cat / by Michaela Muntean; pictures by Bari Weissman; music by Duncan Morrison. — North American library ed.
        p. cm. — (Parents magazine read aloud original)
    Summary: An orange and white striped cat causes a notorious grump to change his ways.
    ISBN 0-8368-0886-X
    [1. Cats—Fiction. 2. Behavior—Fiction. 3. Old age—Fiction.] I. Weissman, Bari, ill. II. Title. III. Series.
    PZ7.M92901  1993
    [E]—dc20                                                                    92-31107

This North American library edition published in 1992 by Gareth Stevens Publishing, 1555 North RiverCenter Drive, Suite 201, Milwaukee, Wisconsin 53212, USA, under an arrangement with Parents Magazine Press, New York.

Printed in the United States of America

1 2 3 4 5 6 7 8 9 98 97 96 95 94 93

# The Old Man
## and the
# Afternoon Cat

by Michaela Muntean
pictures by Bari Weissman
music by Duncan Morrison

Gareth Stevens Publishing • Milwaukee
Parents Magazine Press • New York

To my sisters and brothers—M.M.

To Ron, Cynthia,
and their new baby—B.W.

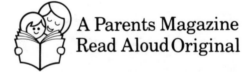
A Parents Magazine
Read Aloud Original

Every morning, the old man woke up
just as the sunlight began
peeking through his window.

He heard the birds singing.
He felt the gentle breezes blowing.
What a lovely way to start the day!

7

"Blech!" said the old man
as he sat up in bed.
He hurried to put on
his sunglasses and earmuffs.
"I hate sunlight and gentle breezes.
But most of all, I hate the sound
of birds singing."

9

Then the old man made his
favorite breakfast of burnt toast,
extra-hard boiled eggs and a big glass
of yucca berry juice to wash it all down.

"Harump," he said, when he finished.
"Now it is time for my grumbling exercises."

He grumbled as he washed the dishes.
He grumbled as he brushed his teeth.

He grumbled as he put on his
itchiest pair of itchy underwear.

Now it may seem to you that
there was nothing the old man liked.
But that is not true.
He liked to sing grumpy songs.
His favorite was, "I Hate Birthdays,"
which he wrote all by himself.

Here is how it goes in case
you are in a very grumpy mood
and would like to sing along:

# I HATE BIRTHDAYS

## by The Old Man

*I hate birthdays, I hate spring.*
*I hate almost everything.*
*I can be nasty, mean and grumpy.*
*I like to sleep on a bed that's lumpy.*
*I'm all alone, there's no one but me.*
*No one that I think about,*
*no one that I see.*
*No one to ask me, "How was your day?"*
*I'm all alone and I like it that way!*

After singing his song,
the old man was ready for his
outdoor grumbling exercises.
His neighbors were used
to his grumbling.
They just smiled and said, "Good day."
"Harump," the old man answered and
grumbled all the way to the park.

At the park, the old man sat far away
from everyone else to read his newspaper.
Then, he sat very quietly and waited.

Now, if you were sitting and waiting
as quietly as the old man,
you would hear it ...
a soft *pat-pat-pat,*
followed by a gentle crunch of leaves.

And if you were sitting
very, *very* quietly,
without a sneeze, or a cough,
or a rustle of a paper,
you would hear a soft and tiny
purring sound.

"Ah," said the old man.
"So you are back again."

And with that, up jumped
an orange and white striped cat.

19

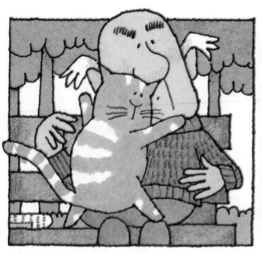

Cats can take a long time
to get comfortable sometimes,
so the old man waited quietly
until the cat had snuggled just right.

Then the old man's chin dropped to
his chest and he began to snore.
And all afternoon they sat together,
the old man and the cat,
taking their afternoon nap.

21

When the cat woke up and stretched,
the old man woke up and stretched too.

Then they both went wherever it was
they had to go until the next afternoon.

But one day something strange happened.
The old man waited as quietly as usual.
He waited until all the mothers
took their babies home.

He waited until the man who sells
hot dogs and popcorn went home.

He waited until the sun went down
and the lights of the town
winked on in the darkness.
Finally, the old man went home.

The next day, the same thing happened.
"I wonder," said the old man,
"what has happened to my afternoon cat."
Then the old man began to worry.
He worried so hard that
he completely forgot about grumbling.

Finally, the old man knew what to do.
He drew a picture of the afternoon cat.
This is what it looked like:

The old man showed his picture
to everyone in the neighborhood.
"That's my morning cat!" said the grocer.
"I give him a fish tail every morning,
but I haven't seen him for days."

"Hmmm," said the baker.
"I can't be sure without my glasses,
but I think that's my lunch cat.
I give him a saucer of milk every day
at noon, but he's been gone for two days."

The school children knew him too.
"That's our after-school cat!" they cried.
"We give him pieces of our leftover lunch."

"My, my," said his neighbor, Mrs. McHatty.
"That's my evening cat.
I give him a cup of warm milk every night,
but I haven't seen him lately.
I hope nothing is wrong."

"If he's a stray," said the policeman,
"he was probably taken to The Cat Home."

31

The old man ran there as fast as he could.

CAT HOME

Sure enough, there was the orange and white
striped cat, who purred a soft and tiny purr
when he saw the old man.

33

The woman in charge gave the cat
to the old man.
"You will need a tag for him," she said.
So the old man waited patiently
while the woman made the tag.

34

It said:

This is not a
stray cat.
He belongs to the
old man
and the old man
belongs to
him.

And with that, the old man and the cat went home.

Now every morning, the old man
and his cat visit the grocer.
She gives the cat a fish tail while
she and the old man have a cup of tea.

At noon, they visit the baker.
The old man and the baker share
a strawberry tart while the cat
has his saucer of milk.

Every day after school, the children share their leftover lunches with the cat and toss a ball with the old man.

And in the evenings, the old man chats
with his neighbor, Mrs. McHatty, while
the cat laps up his cup of warm milk.

The old man is so happy that he has
almost stopped grumbling completely.
Now he only grumbles
if he runs out of his favorite cereal,
or he can't find his socks,
or if it rains on the day
he wanted to go to the zoo.
But everyone grumbles about
those kinds of things sometimes,
because they're grumbly things.

Why, the old man even wrote a new song.
Here is how it goes, in case you
are in a very happy mood and
would like to sing along:

42

# I LIKE BIRTHDAYS

### by The Old Man

*I like birthdays, I like spring.*
*I like almost everything.*
*I like to smile and laugh and giggle.*
*I like to dance and hop and wiggle.*
*There's so many people*
*and places to see.*
*We are very busy, my cat and me.*
*We talk and visit and chat all day.*
*My afternoon cat and I like it that way!*

*(Meow)*

43

# Notes to Grown-ups

## Major Themes
Here is a quick guide to the significant themes and concepts at work in *The Old Man and the Afternoon Cat:*

- People's need for both solitude and companionship
- Moodiness and what it's like to change moods
- Having routines to give structure to our lives

## Step-by-step Ideas for Reading and Talking
Here are some ideas for further give-and-take between grown-ups and kids. The following topics encourage creative discussion of *The Old Man and the Afternoon Cat* and invite the kind of open-ended response that is consistent with many current approaches to reading, including Whole Language:

- Encourage kids to invent their own stories about friendship. They may be about "people" friends or "pet" friends. What are the different things we do that are more fun done together?
- What about being alone? Are there times when, like the old man, you, too, would rather be away from others?
- Why is the old man so grumpy? What things in your life make *you* feel grumpy? Children need to know that it's okay to be moody and out of sorts. Talk about what it often takes to get back into a good mood.
- The old man, the cat, and all the other people in this story have routines that give their days structure and, it seems, some measure of meaning. Talk about the routines that we have and how much we depend on them. How would our days seem if we didn't brush our teeth or have meals at set times of the day? How do kids feel on weekends when these routines are altered? How do they feel when they must return to their routines on Monday?

# Games for Learning

Games and activities can stimulate young readers and listeners alike to find out more about words, numbers, and ideas. Here are more ideas for turning learning into fun:

## "Playdough Snake" Path to Reading

One big step on the path to reading is to learn the letters, not just by their names and what they look like, but also by how they are shaped and arranged in space. A multisensory approach, using tactile and kinesthetic experience as well as visual and auditory cues, helps children learn more quickly. It also gives them a greater sense of connection with what they're learning. So when you show your child a letter and say its name, it is also helpful if your child can *feel* that letter at the same time.

One way is by making "playdough snakes." Roll playdough or clay into long ropes and then shape them into letters as you say the letter name. Your child may want to copy yours, or trace it by laying her or his "snake" on top of the playdough letter you have made. Making the letters of your child's name is a good way to start; more experienced children may wish to make words, like *dog* and *cat,* and then "illustrate" them by making playdough animals to match.

Numbers are also easy to make with "playdough snakes." You and your child can extend this activity by making the correct number of playdough balls to match each number your child makes. This is a good way to introduce the numerical concept behind the number symbol.

For long car rides, or any time when you and your child must sit and wait quietly, tracing letters on each other's back is a good guessing game. With your finger, slowly trace a letter your child knows onto her back and ask your child to guess its name. If your child cannot guess after three tries, trace it on her knee so that she can see what you were doing, and then let your child try to stump you by "writing" a letter on *your* back. You only get three chances!

# I LIKE BIRTHDAYS

## by The Old Man

## About the Author

A friend who could no longer keep her cat once asked MICHAELA MUNTEAN to care for it. Ms. Muntean always loved cats, and so she was happy to take Gaspar. Gaspar became very much at home with Ms. Muntean, waking her in the morning, curling up in her lap, spending lazy afternoons lying in the sun. "You can't ever really *own* a cat," Ms. Muntean says. "But it's a lot of fun when one comes to live with you."

Michaela Muntean is the author of many well-loved children's books, including *The Very Bumpy Bus Ride* and *A Garden for Miss Mouse*.

## About the Artist

BARI WEISSMAN has a black-and-white cat named Oboe. Ms. Weissman says that most of the time Oboe just sleeps. But when he isn't sleeping, he's grumbling. "He's the grumbly one in our household," she explains. He grumbles for his food, he grumbles to be let outside, he grumbles for a hug. "But when he gets what he wants," Ms. Weissman says, "he stops grumbling and purrs."

Bari Weissman's bright and bold illustrations have enlivened many picture books, including *Golly Gump Swallowed a Fly*.